The Small and Tall Ball

Frank J. Sileo, PhD ILLUSTRATED BY Katie Dwyer
FOREWORD BY Billie Jean King

The Small and Tall Ball
Copyright © 2023 by Frank J. Sileo

Published by:
PESI Publishing, Inc.
3839 White Ave
Eau Claire, WI 54703

Illustrations: Katie Dwyer
Cover: Katie Dwyer
Editing: Jenessa Jackson, PhD
Layout: Katie Dwyer, Amy Rubenzer

ISBN 9781683736172 (print)
ISBN 9781683736196 (ePDF)
ISBN 9781683736202 (KPF)

PESI Publishing
pesipublishing.com

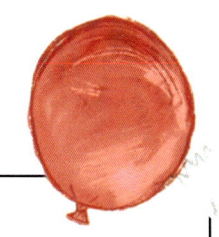

Dedication

To my cousin Mary Jo,
for being the first
editor in my life.
To my cousin Albert,
for always believing in me.

—FJS

✴ Foreword ✴

The Small and Tall Ball is a heartwarming story that teaches the importance of accepting and including each and every person, no matter who they are or what their family looks like. Every adult parent, caregiver, friend, and family member can read this book with the children in their lives to initiate conversations about what it means to welcome and celebrate the wonderful differences in all of us.

Dr. Frank J. Sileo's newest children's book places diversity, inclusion, and equality front and center for young children to understand and appreciate so they can explore them in their own lives. With beautiful illustrations by Katie Dwyer, this book is a wonderful way to have important conversations and reach the hearts and minds of young children.

Our children are our future. We can stand beside them and help them as they transform the words on these pages into actionable steps. When children understand and embrace equality, diversity, and inclusion, we are *all* winners!

✴ Billie Jean King

former world #1 professional tennis player, one of the first well-known openly gay athletes, and activist for equality, diversity, and inclusion

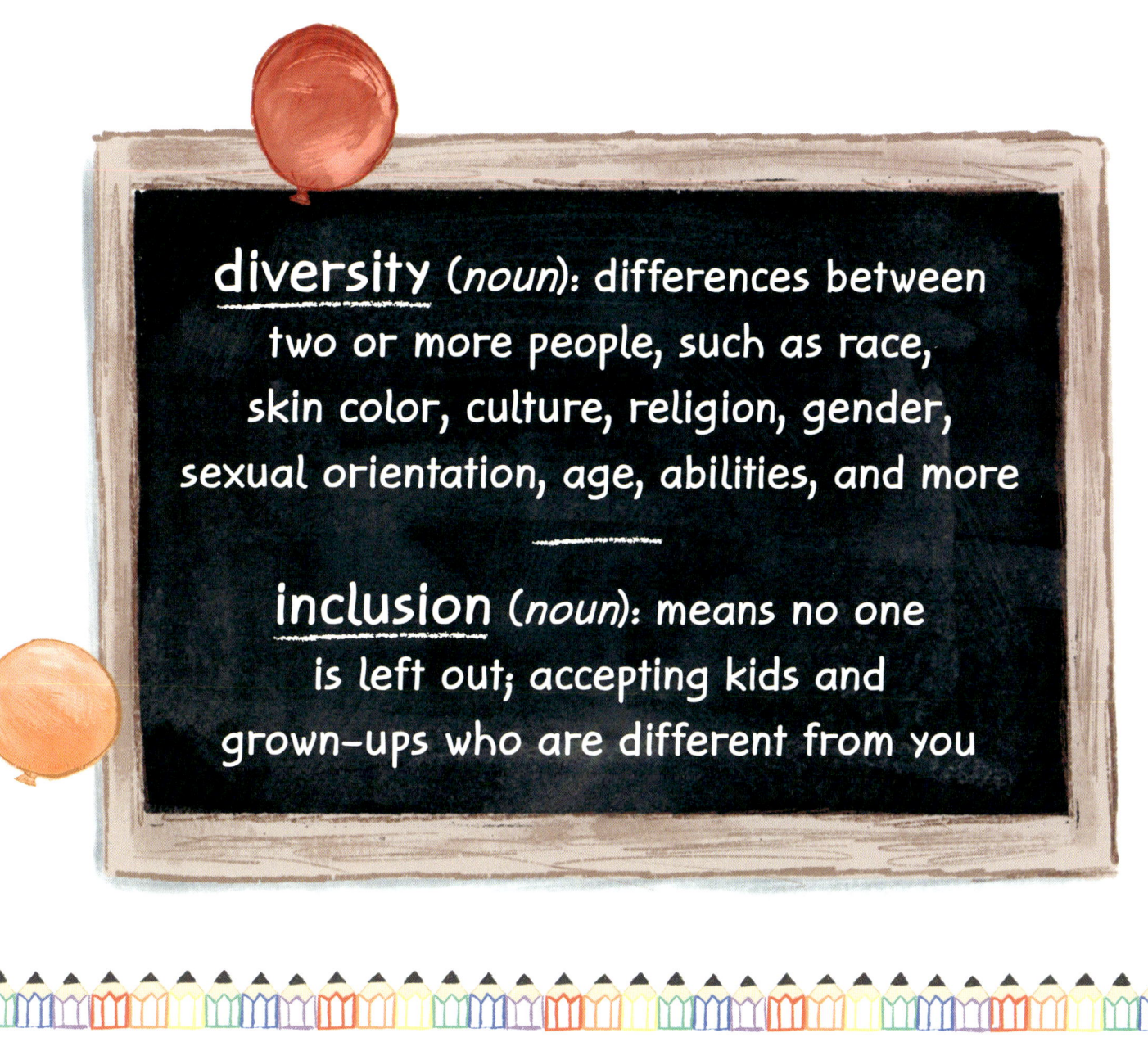

diversity (*noun*): differences between two or more people, such as race, skin color, culture, religion, gender, sexual orientation, age, abilities, and more

inclusion (*noun*): means no one is left out; accepting kids and grown-ups who are different from you

Mrs. Parker's class chattered happily as they blew up balloons and cut streamers. This Friday the class was hosting the annual mother-son and father-daughter dance.

"I'm so excited to wear my purple dress," Abby said.
"My mom bought me a new suit," Liam announced.

Oliver watched from his desk. He wasn't in a good mood. "What's wrong, Oliver?" Logan asked. "Aren't you excited about the dance?" Oliver shook his head. "I'm not going," he whispered. "Why not?" Abby asked, twirling around the table.

"I can't go to the mom and son dance because I have two dads,"
Oliver explained. "And there is no dad and son dance."
"I'm sorry, Oliver. I wish you could come!" Logan said.

Valentina reached over to Oliver. "I can't go to the dance either. My dad is in the military, and he's out of the country."

"What? This is NOT fair!" Emily shouted.
Mrs. Parker heard Emily shouting and came
over to find out what was wrong.

"Oliver can't go to the dance because he has two dads, and Valentina can't go because her dad is away," Emily told Mrs. Parker.

Costa was listening from the other table and said, "I can't go either. I live with my grandparents. It's a mom and son dance, not an abuelita and nieto dance."

"Why can't we have a dance that includes everyone?" Emily asked. "Yeah! Then Valentina could bring her mom instead of her dad, and Oliver could bring both his dads!" Liam added.

Oliver thought about how nice it would be to have his family included. His dads were so fun. He knew he'd have a great time with them.

"Could I bring my abuelita?" Costa asked.
"You could bring anyone who is special to you," Logan said.
"A mom or a dad. A grandpa or an aunt.
A coach or a family friend."

Oliver smiled. This idea was starting to sound better and better.

Mrs. Parker sat down on Oliver's desk to think.
"I don't see why not," she said finally.
"But the dance *will* need a new name. What should we call it?"

"How about the Small and Tall Ball?" Oliver suggested.
Abby giggled, "That rhymes!"
"I like it," Valentina said. "The grown-ups are tall and we are small."

"Yeah, but what's a ball?" Liam asked.
"A ball is a fancy word for a dance," Emily explained.

Valentina grinned and stood up. "A small and tall ball for all!"
"That rhymes too!" Abby said. This time, everyone started laughing.
They were *all* feeling good about the dance now.

"You know," Oliver said, picking up a glue stick, "I think this poster could use more glitter!"

On Friday night, families started arriving for the ball.

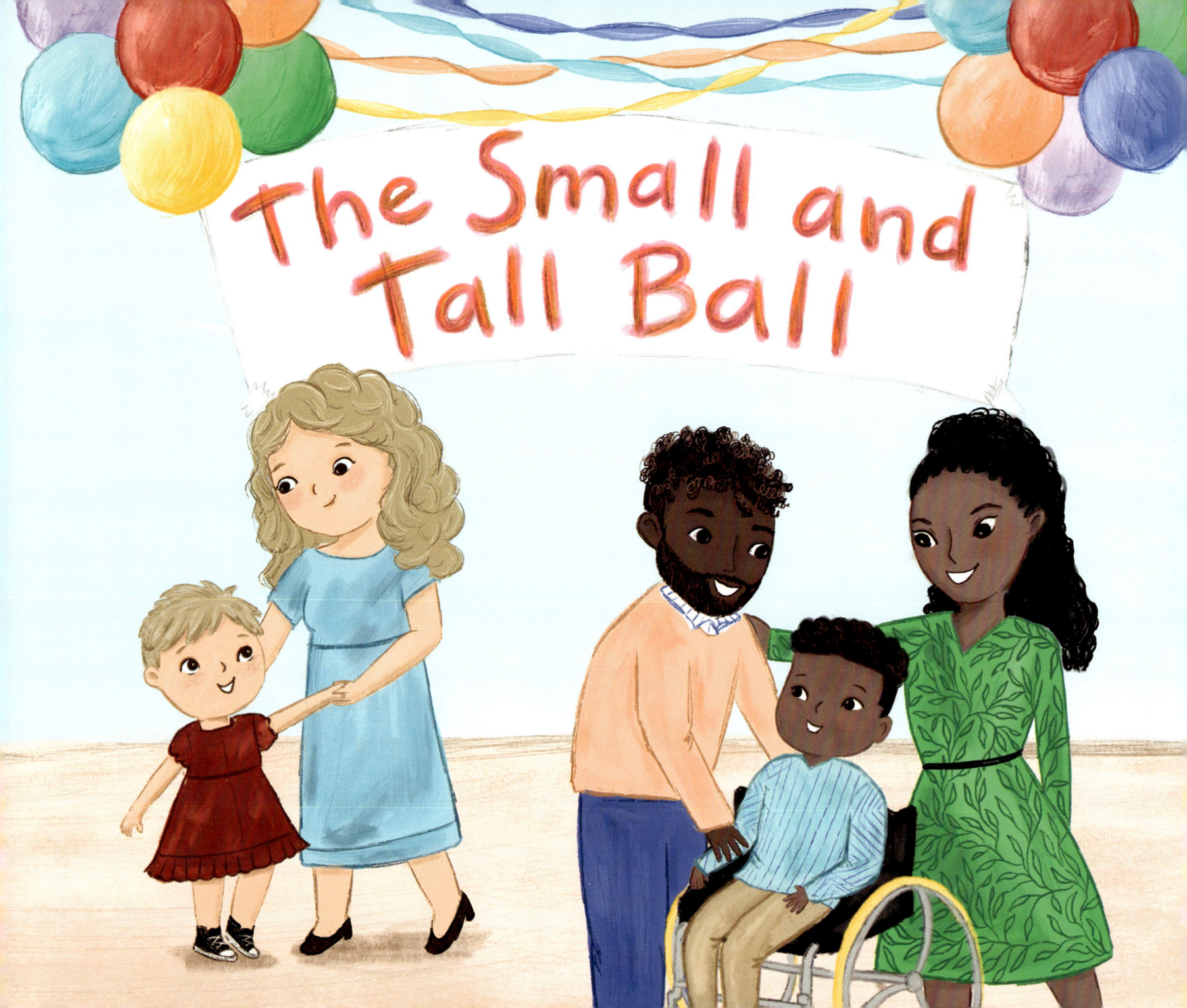

The Small and Tall Ball

Oliver beamed as he and his dads
entered the gym in matching suits.
Valentina waved at her mom,
then asked Oliver to dance.

All night long, the kids danced with their special someone and with each other. There were slow dances, fast dances, and group dances. It didn't matter if you could dance well or had two left feet.

As the ball was ending, Oliver gathered his friends.
"Thanks for making sure my family was included tonight.
Being left out is never fun."

Oliver's friends grinned. It had been a special night for those small *and* those tall! Everyone was welcome and everyone was included.

Note to Parents and Caregivers

It is wonderful that we live in a world of diversity! It gives children an opportunity to interact with people of different races, cultures, abilities, religions, gender identities, sexual orientations, and more. It also allows them to encounter diverse family structures. Unfortunately, even though our world is diverse, it is not always inclusive. Individuals are often excluded from access to housing, employment, sports participation, health care, and more based on these characteristics.

To raise accepting, respectful, compassionate, empathic, and open-minded children, it is important to teach them to embrace diversity at an early age. To teach them to love and value other people who are not like them. To instill the idea that differences are to be celebrated within families and throughout the world. To help them understand that inclusion is a universal human right. When children embrace diversity and inclusion, it creates healthier and happier homes, classrooms, communities, and workplaces—and a greater world.

My goal in writing this book is to help you educate the children in your life on the importance of inclusion and to foster conversations with them regarding the diversity of families. Reading this book with your child will create a wonderful bonding experience and will afford you the opportunity to answer questions and initiate discussions regarding families that are similar and dissimilar to your own, including LGBTQ+ families, grandparent families, military families, and blended families, among others.

Here are some more ways that you can teach your child about these topics:

Be a role model: Your child not only listens to your words but also observes your actions. As a caregiver, you can model an inclusive attitude. Reflect on your beliefs and behavior, including the biases and prejudices you hold. We all have them—the important thing is to identify, face, and overcome them. Ask yourself: "What are my thoughts and feelings about diversity and inclusion?" "How do I celebrate diversity within my family?" Make sure that your language is inclusive and that you use appropriate pronouns. Above all, always back up your words with actions.

Connect with others: Simply encountering a wide variety of people—both in their lives and in media (such as this book)—helps children understand how wonderfully diverse our world is. They learn that the way their own family looks, acts, and views things isn't the only way a family can be. Ask yourself: "How often does my child see and interact with people from different cultures? Different family structures? Members of the LGBTQ+ community? People with different skin colors? Various religions? Different abilities?" Try to expose your child to different places, people, cultures, and families.

Talk to your child: Children are naturally curious and will ask questions, so talk to them about diversity openly! Young children will need explanations that are honest, age-appropriate, and conveyed in a concrete manner. For example, if your child asks, "How come she has two moms?" you can explain that some families have two moms, just as some families have one mom, a stepmom, or no mom. Talk about different kinds of families and emphasize that what matters most is that family means being loved and cared for.

In addition, encourage your child to share their thoughts and feelings about diversity with you. After reading this book, you might ask, "What do you think about Oliver having two dads?" or "What are your thoughts about Costa bringing his abuelita to the dance?" Remember that communication is a two-way street—it involves both talking and listening. Create a safe, trusting, and open space where your child feels like they can be heard.

Help your child be empathic: It hurts to be left out at the lunch table, during a game, or at a social function. It can make people feel unwanted, unloved, and unworthy. Help your child understand what other people may be feeling when they are excluded. When children can better empathize with the experiences of others, it can prompt them to include those who may be marginalized or on the periphery of the social circle.

To facilitate these conversations, you might ask your child, "How do you think Oliver felt when his family wasn't included?" or "How did the children in Mrs. Parker's class make the dance more inclusive?" You can also make connections to your child's own life by asking about times when they were excluded from something, including how it made them feel. If you find that your child is struggling emotionally or behaviorally because of exclusion or social bullying, or if you need additional parenting support, it may be advisable to seek a consultation with a licensed mental health professional who can provide guidance and help.

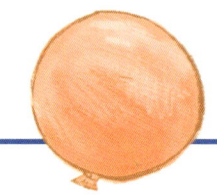

About the Author

Frank J. Sileo, PhD (he/him) is a licensed psychologist and the founder and executive director of The Center for Psychological Enhancement in Ridgewood, NJ. A Fordham University graduate, he works with children, adolescents, adults, and families. Since 2010, he has been consistently recognized as one of New Jersey's top kids' doctors. He is the author of fifteen children's books, which have received various prestigious book awards and have been translated into four languages. He also wrote an award-winning parenting book about raising chronically medically ill children. Dr. Sileo speaks across the country, has published in numerous peer-reviewed journals, and is a go-to psychologist in the media. Learn more at drfranksileo.com. You can follow him on Facebook, Twitter, and Instagram @drfranksileo.

About the Illustrator

Katie Dwyer (she/her) is a children's book illustrator living in the magical woods of Asheville, North Carolina, with her husband and three wildlings. She loves illustrating stories that teach valuable lessons while adding a twist of whimsical charm. When she's not drawing or painting in her studio, she can be found drinking iced matcha lattes with her nose in a book or watching a good movie. Visit her at katiedwyerillustrations.com or on Instagram @katiedwyer.illustrations.